Roger Hurn used to be an actor in 'The Exploding Trouser Company'. He has also appeared on 'The Weakest Link' on TV – and he won!

Now he spends his time writing and telling stories. His scariest and spookiest experience came when he went to an old ghost town in the Wild West of the USA. This gave him the idea for **Spook Squad**.

He hopes you enjoy reading the Spook Squad's adventures as much as he enjoyed writing them.

Spook Squad
The Beast of Hangman's Hill
by Roger Hurn
Illustrated by Peter Richardson

Published by Ransom Publishing Ltd.
Radley House, 8 St. Cross Road, Winchester, Hampshire
SO23 9HX, UK
www.ransom.co.uk

ISBN   978 184167 071 3
First published in 2012
Reprinted 2012

SPOOK SQUAD

The Beast

of

Hangman's Hill

by Roger Hurn

Ransom

DEAD END JUNCTION

Vlad the Bad's Castle

THE GHOST TRAIN RAILWAY

THE ISLE OF FRIGHT

GHOULS' GRAVEYARD

It's the dead centre of Otherworld!

THE WRAITH PITS
They really are the pits!

THE HAUNTED PYRAMID
Your mummy warned you about this place

HERE THERE BE DRAGONS

BANSHEE BAY
Where the wind never stops howling!

They sleep in the day and fight knights!

Otherworld

GOBLIN GULCH
The home of
messy eaters

FANG MOUNTAINS
You'll say 'Fangs for
nothing' if you try to
climb them

KRAKEN LAKE

Swim at
your
own risk!

SPOOK CITY

THE ZOMBI RIVER

WEREWOLF WOODS
Avoid when the
moon is full!

Otherworld

Where is Otherworld?

> The far side of a shadow.

Who lives there?

> Ghouls, ghosts, long-leggedy beasties and things that go bump in the night.

Why do the creatures who live there come to our world?

> To make mischief.

Rhee the Banshee answers readers' questions.

How do they get here?

They slip through secret gateways when you're not looking.

Can humans go to Otherworld?

Yes, but they shouldn't.

Why not?

Because they never come back.

Why not?

Trust me – you really **DO NOT** want to know!

Meet The SPOOK SQUAD

Emma

FYI: She spends her life getting hold of the wrong end of the stick.

Loves: Getting the point.

Hates: Muddy sticks.

Fact: She doesn't like vampires – she thinks they're a pain in the neck.

Roxy

FYI: Don't call her 'Ginger' – unless you want to eat your dinner through a straw.

Loves: Being a strawberry blonde.

Hates: Seeing red.

Fact: She reckons cannibal goblins are messy eaters, so she won't be joining their fang club.

Nita

FYI: This girl gets gadgets. Give her a paper clip, a rubber band, a tin can and an A4 battery and she'll rig up a gizmo that'll blow your gran's pop socks off.

Loves: Fixing things.

Hates: Fixing it – if it ain't broke.

Fact: Nita has invented ghost-proof wheels for her bike. They don't have any spooks!

Leena

FYI: If she was any sharper you could use her to slice bread.

Loves: Big words.

Hates: Small minds.

Fact: She prefers whatwolves and whenwolves to werewolves.

Aunt Rhee

FYI: Rhee's not the kind of aunt who gives you a woolly jumper for Christmas.

Loves: Walking on the wild side.

Hates: Things that go bump in the night.

Fact: Rhee is just too cool for ghouls.

Rattle

FYI: Rattle says he's a poltergeist. He thinks poltergeists are posher than ghosts.

Loves: Boo-berry pie and I-scream.

Hates: People who sneak up behind him and shout BOO!

Fact: Rattle's only happy when he's moaning.

Interview with a Banshee

Aunt Rhee answers readers' questions.

Are you really the Spook Squad's auntie?

No, I'm a banshee.

Aren't banshees evil?

No way! You've been reading too many horror stories.

Do you ever moan like a banshee?

Only if the Spook Squad don't do their homework.

Why do you use a sharp stick when you fight monsters?

I want them to get my point.

Why do the Spook Squad call you 'Aunt' Rhee?

Well, it's better than 'Gran'! Actually, it all came about when I first met the Spook Squad. But that's another story for another day.

The Snard

Description: Your worst nightmare – with extra teeth.

Strength: It can bite through steel.

Weakness: It suffers from hay fever.

Likes: Eating people.

Hates: Flowers.

Favourite food:
Beans (Human beans!)

What to do if you see a snard: Run!

What not to do if you see a snard:
Invite it home for dinner.

Scream Scale Rating:
It's a Hairy Scary!

Prologue

There is a house on Hangman's Hill. It's called The Old Tower. It is surrounded by dark woods.

A creature lurks by the trees. It is a creature from your worst nightmare's nightmare. It lifts its snotty snout and sniffs the air. It growls. It knows its prey is close.

And it is hungry ... very hungry. Drool runs down its jaws. Somehow you just know it's going to be a messy eater.

A light goes on in a window of The Old Tower. The creature sees a gang of girls come into the room. The creature's lips curl back into a smile that could turn a supermarket milk display sour.

It slips silently through the darkness towards the Tower, like the bogey man – only with extra bogeys!

Chapter One

Hunting the Snard

The Spook Squad were at Aunt Rhee's house. They were bored. No strange visitors had slipped across the gateway between the worlds for ages.

'Come on, guys,' said Emma. 'I guess we'd better do our maths homework.'

Roxy, Leena and Nita all groaned.

'No way,' said Leena. 'I'd rather be out hunting vampires!'

Nita and Roxy nodded in agreement.

'Hey, what do you get if you cross a vampire with a teacher?' asked Roxy.

The girls frowned and shook their heads. 'Don't know,' said Leena. 'What do you get?'

'Lots of blood tests!' cackled Roxy. 'Geddit?!'

'Oh ha ha,' said Emma. 'Actually I don't mind maths – it's history I can't do.'

'Why's that?' asked Nita.

Emma sighed. 'Because the teacher keeps asking me about things that happened way before I was born! It's *sooo* not fair.'

'Oh Em,' said Nita. 'Sometimes you're as dim as an energy-saving light bulb!'

Before Emma could reply, Rhee burst into the room. She was definitely not happy. The girls felt a tingle of excitement. Rhee only looked like this when a new monster was on the loose. They all grinned. Life was about to get a lot more interesting.

'Cheer up, Rhee. You look like my mum when she reads my school report card. Things can't be that bad.'

Rhee stared at Roxy. 'Oh yes they can. There's a snard in the woods!'

Roxy frowned. 'What's a snard? It sounds kind of cute and cuddly.'

Rhee shook her head. 'It's as cuddly as a barbed-wire teddy bear, Roxy. It's a creature from your worst nightmare. It's got a hairy body, bloodshot eyes and long, yellow and very jagged fangs.'

'Yikes!' said Emma. 'I *so* wouldn't want

to be its dentist!'

'And I bet its bite is worse than its bark,' said Leena.

Rhee nodded. 'You've got it. But somehow we've got to convince it to go back to its own dimension and leave this world alone.'

Nita rubbed her hands together. 'No problem, guys. I'll invent a snard-stopping machine. All I need is …'

'You'll do no such thing, Nita,' said Rhee. 'Snards are Trouble with a capital T. This isn't a job for the Spook Squad. I'll deal with this on my own. You girls lock the door and DO NOT open it again until I get back.'

Before the Spook Squad could argue, the banshee grabbed a silver-tipped staff of rowan wood and set off to hunt down the snard.

• • • • •

As soon as Rhee left, there was an ear-splitting crash in the kitchen. The girls spun round. They looked at each other in fright, then dashed into the kitchen.

Smashed plates were everywhere. The table was upended and a ghastly moaning sound was coming from behind it.

Leena put her hands on her hips and tapped her foot. 'It's all right, Rattle, you can come out. The snard isn't here.'

A small poltergeist popped his head over the rim of the table. He looked like a see-through sheet in need of a good wash.

'Yeah, but it will be soon,' he said. 'I can feel it coming this way.' Then he groaned

and whizzed off over their heads to hide in
the attic.

Chapter Two

Run, Spook Squad, Run

'Well, I don't know about you guys, but I'm not staying here like a sitting duck waiting for the snard to come calling,' said Roxy. 'We're the Spook Squad and we eat snards for breakfast.'

'I don't,' said Emma. 'I'm a vegetarian.'

Roxy sighed. 'Yeah, but my point is we can have this snard on toast.'

Emma folded her arms and looked stern.

'I don't care how you cook it, Roxy; I am still not eating it.'

'*Errr* … guys,' said Leena. 'We need a plan – and fast – or the snard will be the one doing the eating.'

Nita pulled her smart phone from her pocket. 'No worries, Lee. I'll just go to *www.mankymonsters.com* and check out the entry for snards. I'll get all the facts and then I'll figure out how we can beat it.'

The Spook Squad all looked eagerly at Nita while she read the words on her screen. Then Nita's face fell. 'This is *so* not good news, guys.'

'Why, what does it say?' asked Emma.

'It says, *'If you see a snard – run!'*

Leena did a double take. 'Is that it?'

'That's it,' said Nita.

Emma pulled a face. 'But I'm wearing sling-backs, not running shoes.'

'Then you had better hope we don't see a snard out in the woods,' snapped Roxy.

Nita shook her head. 'Oh no, Roxy,' she

said. 'If there's one thing worse than seeing a snard – it's *not* seeing a snard.'

Roxy frowned. 'Why's that?'

Nita sighed. 'Because if you don't see the snard you don't run, and if you don't run – you're dead!'

Chapter Three

All Tangled Up

The Spook Squad were stuck. They didn't know what to do. The snard was coming closer to the Old Tower with every passing second, and they had no idea of how to stop it.

'I've got it,' said Leena. 'Let's bolt the doors, turn off all the lights and just keep quiet. With any luck the snard will think nobody's at home.'

Nita shook her head. 'Nope, that's no good. According to *mankymonsters.com*, snards have a fantastic sense of smell. It'll sniff us out for sure. And anyway, do you think Emma could stop chatting for more than 30 seconds? No chance.'

Emma opened her mouth to protest. But, before she could speak, Rattle came zooming into the room. He was carrying something. It dangled beneath him like a jellyfish's tentacles.

'Look what I found in the attic,' he screeched. 'A gigantic fishing net!'

'Brilliant,' said Roxy. 'That's just what we need – *not*! We're trying to catch a snard, not a whale.'

'Oh please yourselves,' said Rattle, as he dropped the net on top of Roxy, Nita and

Leena. The three girls fell to the floor. They were completely tangled up in the net. And the more they tried to free themselves, the more tangled up they became.

Rattle watched them struggle. Then suddenly he turned whiter than a sheet in a 60 degree wash and whooshed off back to the attic. The girls were too busy falling over each other to notice.

'Don't just stand there, Emma. Do something,' said Roxy in a voice as sharp as lemons.

But, at that moment, a shadowy face appeared at the window. It wasn't a human face. Emma screamed. The face vanished.

But then came the sound of claws gouging at the kitchen door.

Chapter Four

Food to Go

The door crashed open and a hairy horror lurched into the kitchen. It looked like a cross between a troll with a really bad belly-ache and that wolf that had issues with Little Red Riding Hood.

The snard stared at the Spook Squad and then it spoke. Drool and spittle splattered everywhere.

'Hello girls,' it growled.

Its eyes fixed on Emma.

Emma froze like a rabbit in a car's headlights. Her brain was screaming at her legs to run, but her legs were just not getting the message.

The creature took a step closer to her and sniffed at her with its long nose.

'You smell good,' it growled. 'You're a little on the skinny side, but I'll crunch your bones and feast on your flesh all the same.'

The creature's long, slimy tongue lolled out of its mouth and it licked its lips.

Emma's eyebrows shot up her forehead like two caterpillars on steroids. She'd had bad days before, but this one was at the top of the heap.

'Leave her alone, you mangy mutt,' Roxy

yelled. 'What's she ever done to you?'

The snard turned to look at the three girls in the net. 'Ah, that's handy,' it said. 'Ready-wrapped food. Well, I do like a take-away meal. So when I've finished eating this one, I'll take you three away and eat you later.'

The other girls in the Spook Squad had often said Emma's mouth was on fast forward while her brain was on freeze frame – but not this time. While the snard was talking to Roxy, Emma grabbed a large vase of flowers from a shelf. She crept up behind the creature and raised the vase up above her head, ready to bring it crashing down on its skull.

'Eat this, mister,' she yelled. 'It's headache time ... Oh rats!'

The heavy vase slipped through her hands and shattered on the stone floor. Emma was left clutching a bunch of limp daffodils.

She slammed her eyes shut. Her terrible day had just got a whole lot worse.

Chapter Five

Flower Power

The snard spun round, took one look at the flowers and cowered back in horror. 'No, keep those things away from me! You'll set my hay fever off and I'll be sneezing for a week.'

Then Rhee burst in. 'He's right, Emma. With a snout the size of his, he'll be pebble-dashing my walls with snot – and that will just wreck my colour scheme.'

'Listen to the old trout,' begged the snard. 'She's got a point.'

'Yeah, and talking of points,' said Rhee, 'how about this one?'

She jabbed the snard in its hairy bottom with her sharp, pointed stick. It opened its jaws to howl.

'Eat my daffs,' yelled Emma, as she stuffed the flowers in its mouth.

That was enough for the snard. It fled back out the door sneezing violently, with Rhee in hot pursuit.

Emma wasted no time in freeing the girls from the net. They scrambled out and flung their arms around her.

'You did it, Emma!' said Roxy.

'You beat the snard single-handed,' said Nita.

'You were awesome,' said Leena.

Emma blushed redder than a beetroot with a sun-tan. 'Well, I did have a bit of help from Rhee,' she said. 'But I guess you could say it was all down to flower power in the end.'

The next Spook Squad adventure is

Ghouls at School

It's a Scream!

Spook Squad's Scary Joke Page

What do you call a lazy skeleton?

Bone idle!

Is it true a werewolf won't hurt you if you run away from it?

It all depends on how fast you can run!

What do you call a pretty, friendly witch?

A failure!